This book belongs to

_____

_____

For Honor and Leon
G.G.

For Ann and her big heart
R.A.

This edition published by Parragon Books Ltd in 2014

Parragon Books Ltd
Chartist House
15-17 Trim Street
Bath BA1 1HA, UK
www.parragon.com

Published by arrangement with Gullane Children's Books

Text © Greg Gormley 2013
Illustrations © Roberta Angaramo 2013

ISBN 978-1-4723-3202-8

Printed in China

Pick Me!

Greg Gormley • Roberta Angaramo

Bath • New York • Singapore • Hong Kong • Cologne • Delhi
Melbourne • Amsterdam • Johannesburg • Shenzhen

It was visitors' day at the dogs' home
and Dog was determined to get
a very special owner.

There were plenty to choose from:
tall, elegant dukes,
sparkling movie stars in gold dresses
and powerful presidents.

So when an **ordinary** little girl smiled at Dog,
he stuck his sniffy nose in the air
and turned his back on her.

But as a great and graceful ballet dancer arrived,
Dog did his best to impress her.

He spun on the tips of his pointy paws . . .

and leaped high into the air.

"Pick me!"

said Dog.

But he landed in a muddy
puddle right up to his tummy.
He looked like he was wearing
chocolate trousers.

The great and graceful ballet dancer
was not impressed at all.

Then along came a famous entertainer.
Dog bounced up and down on a large ball
while balancing a trifle on the end of his nose.

"Pick me!"

said Dog.

But he slipped
and the creamy trifle flew everywhere.
The famous entertainer walked on.

Next, a much admired
conductor appeared.
Dog blew into a slide trombone
while rattling a triangle
with his tail.

"Pick me!"

said Dog.

But the slide trombone
slid in two and Dog's bottom
got stuck in the triangle.
The much admired conductor shook his head.

Finally, a most important artist took a look at Dog.

Dog covered his tail in different colours
then used it like a paintbrush.

"Pick me," said Dog.

But great blobs of paint
spattered everything,
making a terrific mess.

The artist ran away in horror.

Dog felt desperate.
**"No one special
will pick me now,"**
he whimpered.

"Yes, they will,
don't worry,"
a voice said . . .

It was the
ordinary little girl.

She fetched soap and water.
She washed off the mud,
the trifle and the paint.

She slid the trombone
back together, prized the
triangle off Dog's bottom . . .

then she gave Dog a good brush.

"Perfect," she said.

With a great, graceful swoosh, Dog leapt up onto the large ball,
landing flawlessly in the arabesque position.

He bounced up and down
and balanced a fresh trifle on the end of his nose.

He played the slide trombone
and rattled the triangle beautifully with his bottom.

He painted a splendid picture
of a white rabbit with an orange carrot . . .

He did it all at the same time and
he did it all perfectly.

"Bravo!" cried the great and graceful ballet dancer.
"Magnificent!" cried the famous entertainer.
"Incredible!" cried the much admired conductor.
"Inspired!" cried the most important artist.

"Pick me! Pick me!"

Dog looked at all the special people
who hadn't been interested
in a plain old clumsy mutt.

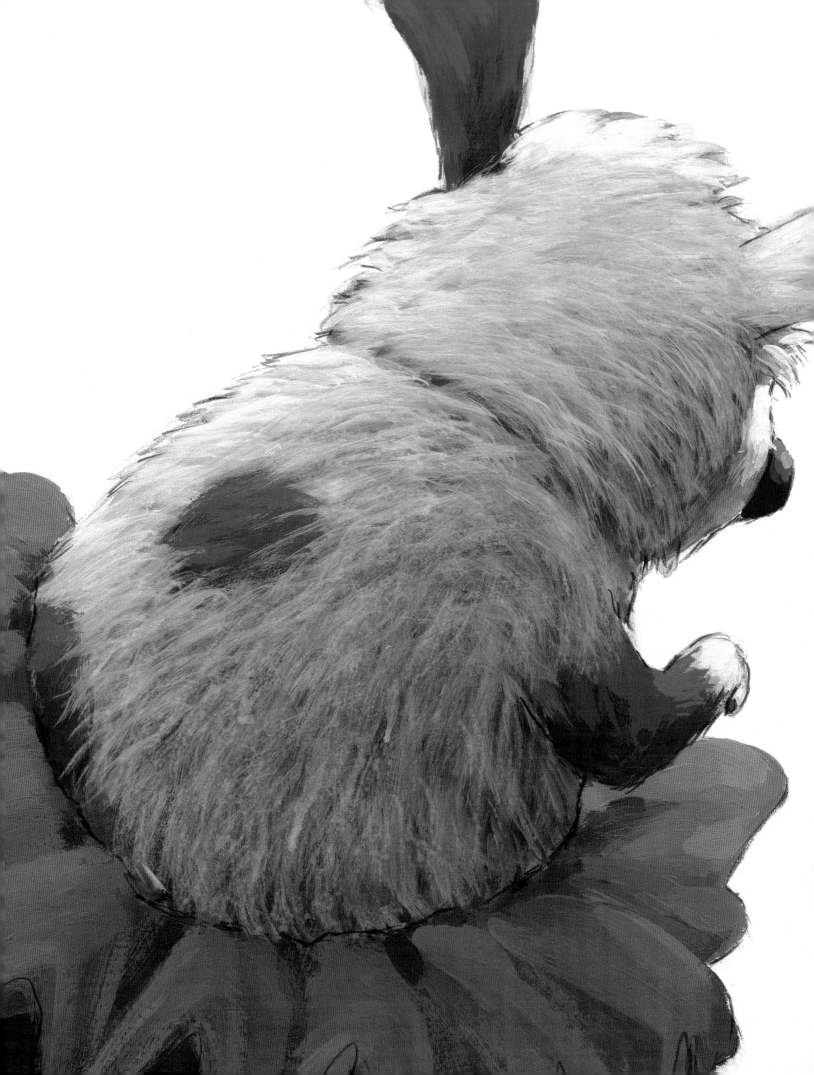

Then he looked at the
very special ordinary little girl.

"Pick me!"
said the little girl
in a quiet voice.

So he did.